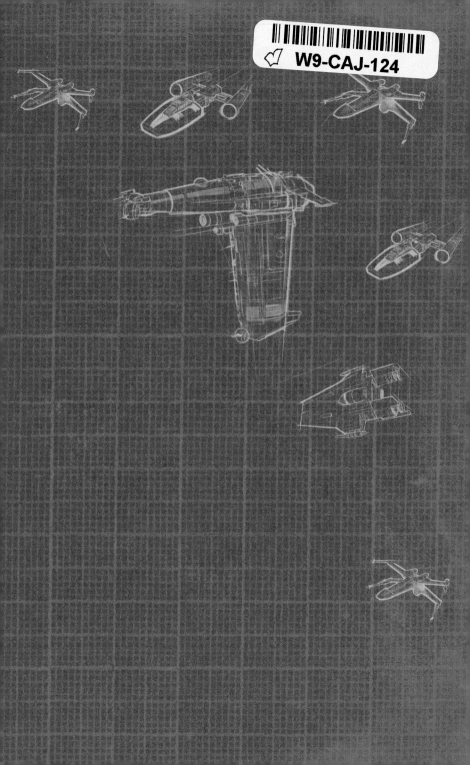

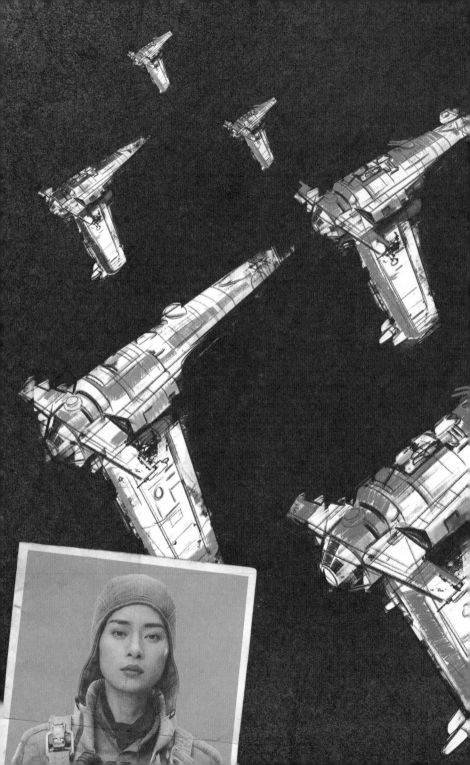

STAR WARS

THE LAST JEDI

BOMBER COMMAND

the journal of Paige Tico

WRITTEN BY JASON FRY

fun
studio
INTERNATIONAL

IMAGINE THIS: You're squeezed into a glass ball that's not a lot bigger than you are. Look up and see a thick door that's magnetically sealed and a durasteel hull. Look down, or to either side, and there's nothing—literally nothing, just black empty space lit only by the bright points of distant stars.

If you let your mind wander you can get confused about up and down and feel like you're floating—or falling. Except you don't have time to let your mind wander.

Because you're _not_ alone out here. There are enemy starfighters all around you firing laser blasts. You're holding the grips of a laser cannon and firing back at them. Every time you fire, the ball shakes, your teeth rattle, and your world gets a bit warmer until the sweat's running down your face and into your eyes.

You can't wipe it away, because you don't dare take your hands off that cannon. And you can't stop firing because if one of those laser blasts gets through the shields, it'll shatter the fragile ball that's THE ONLY THING BETWEEN YOU AND INFINITY.

I'm Paige Tico. I'm a ball-turret gunner aboard a Resistance MG-100 StarFortress bomber, call sign Cobalt Hammer. And this is _my_ story.

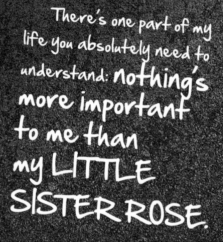

There's one part of my life you absolutely need to understand: **nothing's more important to me than my LITTLE SISTER ROSE.**

She's all I've got left in this galaxy. Our parents are presumed dead, and our homeworld, Hays Minor, was ruined by the First Order. That's how we both wound up fighting for the Resistance.

Rose is five years younger than I am. When I was a little kid, I'd scream for my parents to stop her from following me everywhere. I even threatened to run away from our family's pod and leave her to freeze into an ice cube in the cold darkness outside.

But I got used to Rose, and now I find it hard to imagine a time when I was without her. By the time she was four or five, we were best friends talking about how one day we'd see the galaxy together.

I honestly didn't think we'd ever do it. I thought we'd be lucky to ever travel outside of the Otomok system, but I was wrong. We left as refugees, sent halfway across the galaxy to the Resistance, while our parents fought for our homeworld. We had some clothes, a few credits, and two keepsakes from our parents—medallions of Haysian gold, our planet's most precious ore. The only time I take my medallion off now is in the ball turret, and then I hang it on the gunsight mount of my laser cannon as a good-luck charm.

Rose and I joined the Resistance to stop the First Order from ruining more worlds and wrecking families' lives. We swore we'd do anything to help the cause . . . with one condition. It had to be together. It's like we're two halves of a whole. Without Rose, I feel like a part of me is missing.

Fossil, the commanding officer of our bomber squadron, wasn't happy when she heard she had to find room aboard a StarFortress for my sister. But it worked out because we both showed her what we could do.

I'm a good pilot, and before my days are over I'll be a great one. I've also become a pretty fair shot with a laser cannon.

Rose can't fly the way I can, which has always driven her crazy, but she's a genius with machines. Give her a few minutes to poke around inside something broken, and she'll figure out why it isn't working and how to fix it. Fossil saw what my little sister could do and trained her as a flight engineer . . . something the Resistance needs even more than pilots. But I know the Resistance needs her skills for more than fixing stuck communications arrays and arguing with stubborn droids.

The problem is making Rose realize what she's capable of. My little sister thinks I'm a hero while she's some nobody with a hydrospanner.

ROSE'S TOOLS

What if she figures out a way to let our fleet move across the galaxy undetected? Or invents the machine that lets the Resistance defeat the First Order? Or does something even more amazing that I can't imagine?

I've been thinking about how to get Rose to see that her destiny lies on a <u>different</u> path. But that leaves me with two worries. The first is that she won't be able to accept that. **And the second is that I won't.**

COBALT HAMMER

For now, though, we're together, and sometimes it feels like the closest thing we have to a **home is our bomber, COBALT HAMMER.**

My mother flew an orediger for Central Ridge Mining back home—which was just a decommissioned StarFortress stripped of its military hardware—so I knew my way around Cobalt Hammer the second I set foot on board. There's the flight deck, which is a tube connecting the cockpit, the engines, and the tail-gunner's turret. Then there's the bomb bay, which is a long stalk sticking out from the bottom of the flight deck, with the ball turret hanging off the end.

The bomb bay is a creepy place, typically filled with racks of 1,048 magno-charges. To get to my ball turret, I climb down a tall ladder, past enough firepower to tear a small moon in half, and walk across a narrow catwalk near the bomb-bay doors in the bottom. I know there are all sorts of safety measures to keep those magno-charges from detonating too early, but I still don't like to think about what I'm passing.

I'll never let Fossil know I feel that way. And I'd never tell anyone else on the crew except Rose. Our mother, Thanya, always told us that fears get smaller if you share them with people who care about you. And I'm sure she's right. But this is one fear I'm determined to wrestle with alone.

ZOMBIE LAND

(FOR OXYGEN BREATHERS)

I still can't believe sometimes that I get to be a pilot. I wanted to fly the moment Mama let me sit on her lap in the cockpit of an oredigger. The idea that I could move my hand and have a machine as big as an oredigger obey my commands seemed like a miracle to me. All these years later, it still does.

Back to the bomber . . . if I climb high enough in the bomb bay, I'll come out in the middle of the flight deck— that's what we call the interior of the fuselage. At the top of the ladder is the bombardier's targeting pedestal, which is a computer that takes in everything from our speed and course to magnetic fields and atmospheric conditions, and tells Nix when to drop our payload on the target.

Nix has a good head for numbers, which is needed to make sure the targeting computers take all the variables into account before a drop. He's also cool under fire. When things get intense, though, he does like to yell at Finch Dallow, our _pilot._

You'll find Finch if you move forward from Nix's station. The cockpit is separated from the rest of the flight deck by a bulkhead door. The cockpit's not exactly spacious. There's room for you, the control boards, and the stick. But the view is amazing!

Finch is Cobalt Hammer's regular pilot. He's from Aduba, way out on the edge of Wild Space. He flew crop-dusters and spotter rigs before qualifying for a post in the New Republic's scout service. Being the pilot means he's also the <u>boss</u> during a hop. He not only has to fly, but also has to coordinate operations and decide if a hop needs to be scrubbed if we can't achieve our objectives.

It's a lot to learn, and of course in an oredigger you never had ice and rock shooting back at you. I'm the backup pilot and serve as Finch's relief on long journeys. That's an important aspect of being part of a bomber crew. Everyone has to be able to do at least one other job, in case someone gets hurt or killed during a mission.

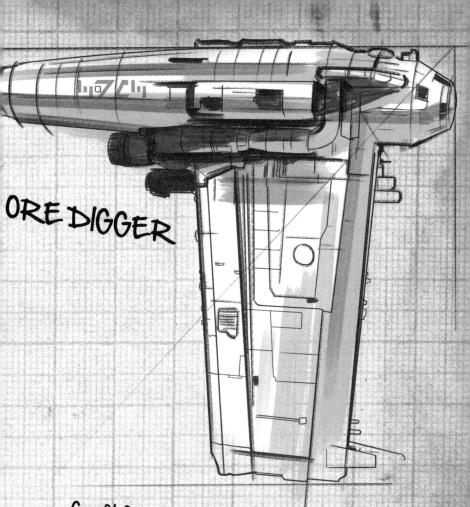

ORE DIGGER

Go aft from the bombardier's pedestal and you reach the flight engineer's station. That's where you'll find my sister, Flight Engineer Rose Tico. Her job includes a little bit of everything: communicating with the rest of the squadron, assisting the pilot with navigation, helping the bombardier with the payload, and keeping Cobalt Hammer in working order.

If you sit at Rose's station, you can feel the thrum of our bomber's engines, since the thrusters are right beneath her. Rose finds the vibration comforting— she says it reminds her that the systems that keep us breathing are doing what they're supposed to do. Past her station, toward the stern, you'll find another bulkhead door and then the tail-gunner's turret.

Cobalt Hammer's regular tail-gunner is Spennie. She's from Coruscant, and has a funny habit of zoning out while we're in hyperspace, listening to ancient broadcasts of space-yacht races. Spennie swears that one day, when things are different, she'll show me and Rose the former galactic capital. I've seen Holos, so I know it's a city that covers the entire planet, but I can't believe such a place is real.

So basically that's our family of crewers, and our home for the Resistance . . . and just about the only home Rose and I have left.

SQUADRON PERSONNEL

FOSSIL

AKA THE OLD LADY, OUR COMMANDING OFFICER. I WAS SCARED TO DEATH OF FOSSIL THE FIRST TIME I MET HER, AND STILL AM. FOR ONE THING, SHE'S HUGE—TOO BIG TO MOVE AROUND IN THE NARROW PARTS OF A BOMBER'S FLIGHT DECK. HER PEOPLE ARE CALLED MARTIGRADES, WITH SHINY SILVER SKIN AND BOOMING VOICES. EVEN THOUGH FOSSIL CAN BARELY CRAM HERSELF INTO A BOMBER, SHE KNOWS EVERY SYSTEM ABOARD A STARFORTRESS AND CAN OFTEN DIAGNOSE WHAT'S WRONG FROM A JUNIOR CREWER'S DESCRIPTION.

HADEEN BISSEL

OUR CREW CHIEF ON D'QAR. CREW CHIEFS ARE SUPPOSED TO BE CRANKY AND MEAN, BUT SOMEONE FORGOT TO TELL HADEEN. HE'S A SWEETHEART. HE LOVES THE BOMBER CREWS AND HIS STARFORTRESSES. I'VE NEVER SEEN HADEEN HAPPIER THAN WHEN HE'S TALKING ABOUT A BOMBER'S ODDITIES. EVERY SHIP IS A LITTLE DIFFERENT, WITH QUIRKS IN STEERING, FUEL CONSUMPTION, OR SOME OTHER SYSTEM. AND ANY PROBLEM WITH ONE OF HIS SHIPS PAINS HIM. HE TREATS A GOUGE IN A BLAST SHIELD LIKE A PARENT WHOSE BABY JUST BUMPED HER HEAD.

VOBER DAND

THE RESISTANCE BASE'S CONTROLLER.
A BIG, BEARDED TARSUNT, DAND IS IN
CHARGE OF GROUND OPERATIONS ON
D'QAR, WHICH MAKES HIM THE LEAST
POPULAR BEING ON THE WHOLE PLANET
MOST DAYS. VOBER HAS TO DECIDE
WHICH SHIPS GET FUEL IF THERE'S A
SHORTAGE, WHICH SQUADRONS GET
SPARE PARTS, AND MAKE A BUNCH OF
OTHER DECISIONS, EACH OF WHICH WILL
MAKE SOMEONE MAD. THE BOMBER
CREWS ALL SWEAR HE FAVORS THE
STARFIGHTER PILOTS OVER THEM. BUT
THEN I'VE OVERHEARD THE FIGHTER
PILOTS COMPLAIN THAT HE DOES
NOTHING FOR THEM BUT EVERYTHING
FOR US. I FEEL SORRY FOR VOBER.

TIGGS KAIGA

TIGGS IS OUR FLIGHT SURGEON. SHE'S A
TALL, SKINNY FAUST WITH NO SENSE OF
HUMOR AT ALL—I MEAN ZERO. YOU
DON'T JOKE WITH TIGGS, BECAUSE SHE'S
THE ONE WHO DECIDES IF YOU GET TO
FLY ON A MISSION OR IF YOU'RE
GROUNDED AND HAVE TO GO SEE HER
BOSS, DOCTOR KALONIA. TIGGS DOESN'T
JUST LOOK JUST FOR PHYSICAL
INJURIES, BUT ALSO EXHAUSTION,
STRESS, OR OTHER AILMENTS THAT
MIGHT CAUSE YOU TO PANIC OR FREEZE
UP DURING A HOP.

BOMBER MISSIONS

The first day of training with our unit on D'Qar, I was sitting in the canteen eating breakfast with a couple of other trainees when a bunch of veteran pilots at the next table started telling stories.

The stories they told were <u>terrifying</u>. Crews killed when a bottom of a rack of magno-charges detonated and blew the clip back up through the fuselage. Crewers who ditched with faulty oxygen gear and suffocated in space. A ball-turret gunner who survived having her bomber blown apart, but was trapped in the ball and eaten alive by mynocks. I sat there in horrified silence with the other trainees and found I'd lost my appetite.

It was rough stuff, but now I understand what they were doing. Everyone in a bomber is depending on everyone else aboard that ship to do their job—and every bomb crew in a squadron is depending on every other crew. If someone's going to freeze up in combat or panic under fire, it's better to learn that on the ground than in space. If you mess up enough simulated missions, the Resistance will find something else for you to do. If you mess up a real mission, people die.

The stories didn't make me quit, so that was one test passed. After that, they checked me out on simulators to see if I could really fly a bomber or if I just wanted to fight the First Order so badly that I'd say anything. Fortunately, all that time flying orediggers for Central Ridge Mining left me well prepared.

A big difference, of course, is that a bomber is under fire from enemy fighters and artillery. The most important lesson I had to learn was to fly in formation. Formation is critical because a lone bomber is easy prey for starfighters. To survive an attack run, you need your fighter escort and the other bombers around you. You combine your defensive fire in overlapping fields to make yourself a much more dangerous target.

The bomber pilots who've flown missions for the New Republic against pirates and local threats told me something else: smart fighter pilots can spot a new crew by circling a formation of bombers once. An inexperienced bomber pilot will ride his or her throttle out of fear of being attacked, drifting out of tight formation. That's the signal for the fighters to swarm, separating that bomber from the others and destroying it. And that will leave a hole in the squadron that they can exploit.

So, we use a number of formations on missions, but the most common formation is two flights of three StarFortresses: a leader and two wings. On the way to the target, we'll often fly with the flights stacked one above the other—one "high" and the other "low." The hardest angle for a bomber to defend against is fighters coming from directly ahead and above, because neither the tail gunner nor the ball gunner can direct fire there. Stacking flights reduces that vulnerability by letting the bombers on top defend those below.

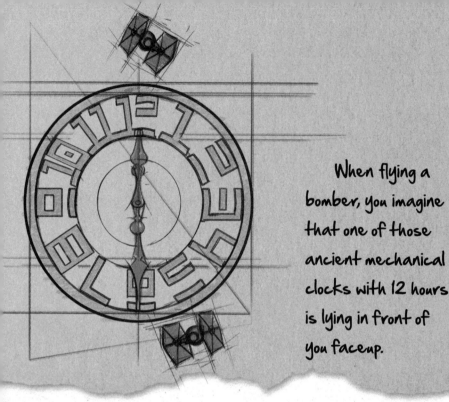

When flying a bomber, you imagine that one of those ancient mechanical clocks with 12 hours is lying in front of you faceup.

A fighter coming from directly in front and above you would be coming from "12 high," and "6 low" would refer to a fighter coming at you from the ground and behind. It takes a little getting used to, particularly if you're from a planet that didn't tell time that way, but after a little practice you know <u>instantly</u> where to look.

There's no safe spot in a bomber formation once laser blasts and concussion missiles start flying, but everyone agrees the most dangerous place is the right wing of the low flight. That spot is nicknamed Medal of Bravery corner.

If I look out from my turret during an attack run, I'm hoping to see Resistance starfighters acting as escorts. Fighters are much more maneuverable than bombers. Unfortunately, the Resistance usually needs its fighters for other missions, leaving us on our own. Without fighters, a bomber has to rely on its guns. Luckily, a StarFortress is <u>far</u> from helpless in that department. The ball and rear turrets have a wide field of fire, and the topside turret has a 360-degree field of fire and is controlled remotely. Bombers also have dual stern guns, "chin" guns beneath the cockpit, and laser cannons at the end of the flight-deck stabilizers. These guns can be fired from a gunner's station, the cockpit, or set to automatic fire.

BOMBERS THROUGH TIME

Defenses are critical, but the most important job for a bomber crew is to get to the target and release the payload, no matter what threats you face. The hardest thing for me to learn as a bomber pilot was that my job was often to do nothing. A StarFortress is big, slow, and awkward. It can't outrun or outmaneuver starfighters.

It takes real bravery to stick to a flight path even as your shields are plummeting to zero and your hull armor is starting to glow red from a torrent of cannon fire.

CRASH PROCEDURE

MANUAL

A hop begins with your crew being summoned to a briefing. It's very rare that we know anything about a mission until a couple of hours before our Forts get into space.

The lead bomber sends data to the rest of the squadron. We follow that Fort all the way to the target. Once the squadron reaches the IP, that's the initial point of the run, you're locked in.

By now, there are going to be enemy fighters all over you and surface-to-air fire if you're attacking a planetary target. There's nothing to do but hold your course and tell the gunners to blast away for all they're worth.

The bombardier will be huddled over his pedestal, making last-minute checks and reviewing any new information transmitted by the illuminator. At two minutes to target, the bombardier will perform a final diagnostic check on the magno-charges and hurry into the bomb bay for any last-minute maintenance required. Every bombardier carries a remote trigger along just in case we reach the target while he or she is busy in the bomb bay.

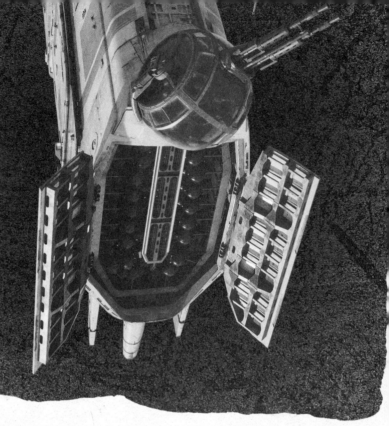

Magno-charges have three built-in safety devices to keep them from detonating prematurely. The bombardier has to arm them by inputting codes from the pedestal or the remote trigger. That activates the fuse mechanism. Magno-charges also have impellers as part of the fuse assembly, which prevents the strike pin from triggering an explosion. These impellers automatically drop off when the bomb has traveled a certain distance. The next step is the last one: the bomb impacts and explodes.

Sometimes fuse mechanisms fail to activate and have to be tripped by hand, requiring the bombardier to climb down and find the faulty magno-charge on the racks. Or a magno-charge may get hung up on one of the racks, in which case the bombardier will either dislodge it and let it drop or disarm it and stow it.

If all goes well, you know the instant the bombs are gone because the bomber lurches as the clip empties. And then all you've got to do is get to safety.

If things go really wrong on the other hand, we have to scuttle and ditch. I've practiced this procedure, but fortunately I've never had to try it for real. But if the choice is between ditching and smashing into a moon aboard a crippled bomber, I'll give it a shot.

Once the order is given to scuttle and ditch, the flight engineer will enter commands that purge the bomber's computer systems of any information about the Resistance: the location of bases, crew records, and stuff like that. Then everyone heads to the nearest working exit. For the four crewers on the flight deck, that's the entry hatch. For me, it's the bomb-bay doors. All of us have bailout kits that contain a parachute, breathing apparatus, a map of the target area, water, concentrated ration bars, medicine, and a directional finder.

None of that stuff will keep you alive in space for very long, and if you do make it to the ground of an occupied planet alive, the First Order will be looking for you.

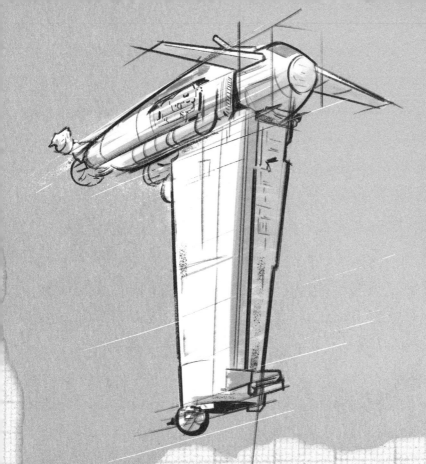

Assuming a fighter doesn't shoot you down and the bomber makes it back to base, you then report to the crew chief and tell him everything his maintenance team needs to know, like drift in the rudder, an overheated deflector shield, a faulty sensor, etc. You never skip this step, ever. Droids are great at finding problems once they occur, but not so great at discovering them before they happen.

After a maintenance check, you report to the interrogation room with the other crews for debriefing with Fossil and other officers. They'll have all the data from the bombers' computers, but they still want to hear from the crews. They treat our impressions of the battle as if they're as important as the targeting data and damage estimates. Each crew can only report on its own little piece of the mission, but talking to all the crews will give Fossil a full picture of how things went.

And then you hit your bunk because by then you're exhausted. The next morning you book time on the simulator to practice what didn't go well, or you check in with Hadeen to see how the repairs are going. And then you wait for the call to the briefing room for the next mission . . . when it starts all over again.

BOMBER SLANG

LIKE EVERY OTHER PROFESSION, BOMBER CREWS HAVE THEIR OWN UNIQUE LANGUAGE. HERE'S THE RUNDOWN:

BANDIT—enemy ship

BIG L—lightspeed

BOFFINS—research & development scientists *Rose would make a top-notch boffin!*

CATCH A PACKET—get hit by enemy fire

CLUTCH—a TIE squadron

COLD NOSE—sensors down

EDGE—an A-wing fighter

EYEBALL—a TIE fighter

FLYING THE SAME VECTOR—thinking the same way

FORTS—bombers

GET LINES—disengage and jump to hyperspace

GRIPE—a mechanical problem

HOP—a mission

ILLUMINATOR—lead bomber that spotlights the target

IP—initial point of bombing run

MPI—mean point of impact

NO DECOR—speak freely without worrying about rank

OLD LADY—squadron's commanding officer *(in our case Fossil)*

OLD LAG—an experienced crewer

PAINTED—scanned by sensors

POINTER—an X-wing fighter

SHOCKER—ion cannon

SPROG—an inexperienced crewer

STICKS—groups of bombs

WANNABES—First Order personnel *(because they deserve it)*

WISHBONE—a Y-wing fighter

ZERO HOUR—mission start time

ADVENTURES

When Rose and I were kids, we loved to tell stories about our future adventures. In one story, we'd belong to a circus bringing joy to sad worlds; then in the next one we'd join a medical team helping animals after some natural disaster. Rose's <u>one condition</u> was that every imaginary place we visited had to be warm, with blue seas and plenty of greenery and two bright suns in the sky.

We've been to planets other than Hays Minor, but I still smile when I see Rose's joy at encountering a new world. I wish we hadn't left home the way we did, and many of the places we visit are troubled, but we're finally seeing the galaxy like we always dreamed of.

Our homeworld, Hays Minor, revolves around binary stars in the Outer Rim's Otomok system. It's a cold and dark little planet, at the very edge of Otomok's habitable zone. Nothing can live on its surface. Outside, you won't find anything but ice and bare rock, beneath a sky that never gets brighter than gray. When we first came to D'Qar, Rose and I needed to wear filtered goggles outside for weeks. We couldn't get used to the light and heat.

Hays Minor's sister world is Hays Major, a gloomy, stormy world that's busy with trade and heavy industry. Hays Major and Minor relied on each other for decades, with Minor sending ore and minerals to Major in return for food, water, and machinery. But that was before the First Order came and took control of Hays Major's industries. Once that happened, it was just a matter of time before they crushed the life out of our homeworld.

The moment we saw a holo-map of the Atterra system, Rose and I were reminded of home. The system's sunlight is the same color . . . I remember it so clearly.

Atterra has three primary worlds: Atterra Primo, Atterra Alpha, and Atterra Bravo. Atterra Primo is a gas giant unsuitable for life, separated from the other two worlds by a chaotic asteroid belt of tumbling rock.

Atterra Alpha and Atterra Bravo are twin worlds with a moon each, and both planets share a single orbit. They're so perfectly balanced that neither planet's gravity affects the other one. Like Hays Major and Minor, Atterra Alpha and Bravo rely on each other.

We made several runs to Atterra Bravo for the Resistance—and took heavy losses doing so. While I like visiting any new planet, Bravo was a spooky place. For one thing, its seas are deadly acid, and I've heard horror stories about what those waters can do to unprotected flesh. Many of Bravo's islands are dotted with towering columns of pumice, and the wind makes an eerie noise as it whistles through these rock formations.

Still, for the people of Bravo, this was home, and they loved their home and vowed to protect it. Like the people of Atterra Bravo, Rose and I were determined to fight when the First Order tried to take our home away.

D'Qar and Atterra were too far apart for easy supply runs in our bombers, so we looked for a base of operations closer to First Order space. Cat, a tech on one of our Forts, said his homeworld of Refnu was in the perfect location.

Refnu reminded me and Rose of home, too, in a way. It was a cold and dark planet, and only warm enough for life because of its dense cloud cover. But Refnu had that same stark beauty I remembered from back home, and that was before we found out the Nefrians had imported snowgrape vines and selakale. For just a moment, holding a snowgrape's sour fruit under my tongue, I could close my eyes and imagine everything that's happened to us was a dream. I'd be at home in our sunroom, ready to get geared up and fly another hop for Central Ridge Mining. That wasn't true, of course. But it was nice to imagine.

Now we're on our way back to D'Qar—the first world where I ever saw a real live animal. Whenever we land here after a mission, I make Rose follow one of the jungle paths with me. After all that time cooped up in a ship, I need to look up at the sun shining through the delicate traceries of the leaves. Or if it's night, I need to hear the chorus of insects . . . the buzz rising and falling based on some pattern only they understand.

The idea of First Order bombs laying waste to D'Qar makes me want to <u>scream</u> . . . or shoot something. When Rose and I made up our stories, we dreamed of a world like it. And despite all the tragedy we've witnessed, I'm so glad my sister and I have been able to see some of what we dreamed of together—and to learn that the galaxy is still an amazing place, full of heartbreaking beauty and wonder.

FATHIER: If you told me I could only see one creature in the galaxy, it would be a fathier. Someday I want to see a fathier race! I wouldn't even bet— I'd just watch!

SONAR SWALLOW:

These were the first real animals I ever saw! Everyone on D'Qar saw them as a nuisance, but I thought they were lovely.

GORGS: I hear Hutts eat these poor beasties alive and right out of the bowl. Yuck!

TOOKAS: Grandma Etta had a tooka before she and Grandpa Storm came to Otomok, and she used to tell me stories about him. I had stuffed tookas as a little girl, but in my games, they were ferocious hunters.

MYNOCK: Spacers hate these guys because they attach themselves to ships and chew power cables and other exposed parts. Even Hadeen thought I was crazy when I said I wanted to see one. It's not their fault their diet consists of energy!

NARGLATCH: These snow cats are found on Orto Plutonia and other worlds. Papa asked if I'd be scared to see a narglatch pride peeking in our observation dome. . . . I wish!

PURRGIL: Purrgil live in deep space and can be hazardous to ships. Finch swears that if he ever spots one during a hop, he'll let me take over the flying and get a closer look.

HAPPABORE: These big beasts live on all sorts of worlds, doing everything from pulling heavy machinery to carrying kings and queens around in howdahs on their backs. What a way to travel!

THE RESISTANCE

I told you how one of Fossil's first lessons was the importance of flying in formation, so each bomber can rely on the ones around it. Well, the Resistance is like that. It's made up of overlapping groups that support each other and depend on each other.

Something I'm still getting used to is that I don't know very much about our overall capabilities—only our t[o] leaders do. That's for a good reason, too. We'[..] be in a lot of trouble if the First Order could discover everything about the Resistance' capabilities by capturi[ng] one bomber crew.

THE RADDUS

THE FLEET: The task force assigned to D'Qar is anchored by General Organa's flagship, a huge Mon Calamari cruiser called the <u>Raddus</u>, and Vice-Admiral Holdo's bunkerbuster, the Ninka. The Raddus has a dedicated hanger that can accommodate four full bomber squadrons. I wish we had that many!

Besides those ships, our task forces include the medical frigate Anodyne and a Mon Calamari cargo frigate, the Vigil. That's about it. We have to get by with whatever General Organa can beg, borrow, or steal from the New Republic, and these days that's nowhere near as much as we need.

What if our task force at D'Qar is all that stands between the First Order and victory?

GROUND TROOPS:

The Resistance has ground units and dedicated commandos, but the biggest surprise to me is that everybody gets infantry training. And I do mean everybody. Rose and I were sent off to a week of boot camp when we arrived. It doesn't matter if you're a pilot, a technician, or ground crew, you also have to be able to pick up a blaster and use it in a fight.

THE LEADERSHIP: The Resistance wouldn't exist without General Organa. It's that simple. She met Rose and I when we arrived from Otomok, and listened quietly while we explained that the First Order had murdered our planet and we had to join the fight. What kind of general has time for a pair of bewildered refugees from the back of beyond? But General Organa goes out of her way to know everybody, and recruited the entire command hierarchy personally, from Ackbar, Holdo, and Statura to Fossil and hot-shot pilots like Poe Dameron.

A GALACTIC FIGHT:

The Rebel Alliance emerged from local groups that rose up to fight the Empire in their home systems and sectors. To fight the First Order, General Organa has gone back to that idea. We don't have enough capital ships or troops to oppose the First Order everywhere, but we can look for ways to make a difference—contributing medicine or blasters, or bringing rebels to Resistance headquarters for a week of commando training. When we discovered what was happening at Atterra, we knew we couldn't respond by invading with a task force. But we were able to help by using our bombers to make supply runs to Atterra. The gear we brought Bravo Rising will let them fight the . And one day I swear we'll do the same thing for the people trying to free Otomok.

I hate the First Order's leaders. I don't say that lightly—Mama always warned that hatred can consume you. They ruined our planet out of greed, and they ordered the killings we saw them try to cover up on Atterra Bravo.

I know that the First Order won't stop. They want to destroy everything the New Republic has built. They have to be stopped, and if I can do even a little to stop them, my life will have been worth it.

But I won't let myself hate everyone in the First Order. For all I know the stormtroopers, pilots, and technicians are just like me and Rose—they found themselves stuck in a situation they never chose. Maybe some of them are looking for a way out of that trap.

This isn't just some fantasy of mine either. Our raid against Starkiller Base succeeded because of our infiltration team, which relied on vital intelligence from a former First Order stormtrooper named Finn.

I hope I get to meet Finn some day and hear his story. He risked his life because his conscience wouldn't let him follow evil orders. Instead, he helped Commander Dameron escape First Order captivity and returned Poe's droid to the Resistance. To me, that's a hero. And we'll win this fight because people like that are out there, even within the First Order.

I have to tell Rose about Finn. She gets s. angry about everything that's happened to us that I worry about her. I think Finn's story is one she needs to hear. We all need hope to get through this fight.

AN ADDRESS TO THE NEW REPUBLIC
SENATE FROM LEIA ORGANA

SOME OF YOU STOOD BESIDE ME IN THE IMPERIAL SENATE WHEN WE SPOKE FOR WORLDS THAT HAD BEEN SILENCED BY PALPATINE'S WAR MACHINE. AFTER THE EMPIRE DISSOLVED THE SENATE, OTHERS OF YOU FOUGHT BESIDE ME IN THE STRUGGLE TO RESTORE FREEDOM TO THE GALAXY. AND ALL OF YOU ARE FELLOW CITIZENS OF A GALAXY YEARNING FOR PEACE AND PROSPERITY. I HOPE YOU WILL REMEMBER THESE BONDS THAT UNITE US AS YOU LISTEN TO WHAT I HAVE TO SAY.

AS A YOUNG SENATOR, I SAW MY HOMEWORLD OF ALDERAAN VAPORIZED BEFORE MY EYES, DESTROYED BY A MURDEROUS MACHINE THAT THE EMPIRE HAD CREATED. THE HORROR OF WATCHING SO MANY LIVES EXTINGUISHED WILL NEVER LEAVE ME. THAT MOMENT CHANGED ME FOREVER, AND MADE ME VOW THAT I WOULD LIVE TO SEE AN END TO WAR AND THE BEGINNING OF AN ERA OF PEACE.

BUT THAT PEACE COULD ONLY BE ACHIEVED THROUGH VICTORY AT ARMS. A NOBLE BUT MISGUIDED FEW SAID THAT THOSE OF US WHO OPPOSED THE EMPIRE SHOULD SURRENDER AND HOPE FOR MERCY FROM PALPATINE, BUT THAT WOULD HAVE SENTENCED THE GALAXY TO MILLENNIA OF TERROR. OUR ALLIANCE NEEDED HOPE—BUT NOT BLIND HOPE.

THE EMPIRE NOW LIES IN ASHES, BUT THE FIRST ORDER HAS RISEN FROM ITS EMBERS. AND IN THE GALAXY'S SHADOWS, ITS LEADERS ARE DIRECTING A CAMPAIGN THAT HAS ONLY ONE GOAL: THE DESTRUCTION OF THE NEW REPUBLIC YOU HAVE WORKED SO HARD TO LEAD.

I WISH I WERE WRONG. I WOULD GLADLY TELL MY DETRACTORS IN THE SENATE THAT THEY ARE RIGHT—THAT I AM AN ALARMIST, A WARMONGER, AND A RELIC FROM THE LAST WAR. BUT THIS ISN'T ABOUT ME. IT'S ABOUT EVIDENCE COLLECTED AT GREAT COST BY BRAVE MEN AND WOMEN WHO SEEK THE SAME PEACE WE ALL DO.

I HAVE COMPILED INFORMATION VITAL TO THE SURVIVAL OF THE NEW REPUBLIC INTO THE GRACE REPORT. I URGE YOU TO READ IT. IT DETAILS SOME OF THE MANY WAYS THE FIRST ORDER HAS VIOLATED THE GALACTIC CONCORDANCE, USING IT AS A SHIELD TO PREPARE FOR WAR.

YOU WILL SEE HOW THE FIRST ORDER HAS CREATED STATE-OF-THE-ART TIE FIGHTERS, ATTACK CRAFT, AND NEW CLASSES OF STAR DESTROYERS THAT NOT ONLY ENFORCE ITS WILL IN FIRST ORDER SPACE, BUT ALSO THREATEN NEUTRAL WORLDS IN THE GALACTIC BORDERLANDS.

YOU WILL READ INTELLIGENCE REPORTS FROM PHERYON, KADDAK, AND SHEH SOAHI AND CAPTURED SURVEYS FROM THE STAR SYSTEMS OF THE UNKNOWN REGIONS, WHERE THE EMPIRE HAS HIDDEN SHIPYARDS, ARMORIES, RESEARCH-AND-DEVELOPMENT LABS, AND ACADEMIES. ALL OF THESE FACILITIES ARE NOW WORKING DAY AND NIGHT ON A MASSIVE MILITARY BUILDUP—ONE FAR LARGER THAN ANYTHING THE FIRST ORDER COULD POSSIBLY NEED TO DEFEND ITS MEMBER WORLDS.

YOU WILL HEAR TESTIMONY FROM REFUGEES WHO FLED FIRST ORDER SPACE TO WARN US OF WHAT LIFE IS LIKE UNDER ITS RULE. THEIR STORIES ARE ABOUT PROPERTY SEIZED, POPULATIONS RELOCATED, CHILDREN KIDNAPPED, AND DISSENTERS EXTERMINATED.

THE FIRST ORDER'S LEADERS ARE MASTERS OF RHETORIC, UNLEASHING TORRENTS OF PROPAGANDA AND FEAR. THIS IS A DELIBERATE STRATEGY DESIGNED TO DISTRACT US FROM WHAT THE FIRST ORDER IS DOING IN SECRET, AND ABOUT WHICH IT IS SILENT.

First Order incursions into New Republic space continue to happen, with the resulting diplomatic protests ignored. The First Order's cooperation agreements with neutral systems are enforced by the business end of blasters. And the First Order's calls to civilize the galactic frontier are a story they tell to cover their colonization of star systems—systems that New Republic observers aren't permitted to visit.

No one, least of all me, wants to see war consume the galaxy again. But war is coming, whether we like it or not. Many senators have demanded that I show them evidence the First Order has violated the Galactic Concordance. This report contains that evidence, and it is irrefutable. I urge you to view it with an open mind, seeing what is there instead of what you wish to see. And then I urge you to ask yourself this question: What if the next irrefutable evidence isn't a message from a friend, but an attack from an enemy?

Should that day arrive, what will you do? And what will you tell the people of the galaxy you swore to defend?

Leia Organa

OUR STORY

All four of our grandparents came to the Otomok system with its first wave of settlers. They'd heard reports of rich minerals beneath the crust of Hays Minor and its sister world, and hoped to strike it rich.

Our father's parents hadn't been here long when they made their first mineral strike, and it was a lucky one—gold smelt. Grandpa Storm and Grandma Etta celebrated by striking the snowgrape medallions that Rose and I still wear. But there were other treasures on Hays Minor. Beneath its frozen surface explorers found an endless labyrinth of caverns. They discovered caves glittering with crystals of every color, and underground lakes warmed by thermal upwells, colonized by tangles of albino snowgrape vines and clumps of selakale.

Most Haysians chose to live underground, in pod clusters. We were lucky—our village's snowgrape vine grew in our family sunroom. Rose and I loved looking at its teardrop-shaped pale green leaves, smelling its spicy blossoms, and eating its fruit.

CRYSTAL CAVES

I remember as soon as Rose could walk she demanded that I make room in the nest of pillows and blankets I'd made in our pod's observation dome for her. You couldn't see the sky from my bed, but a few stars were always visible from the dome, even during the day. At night, the galaxy was spilled out over our heads, like someone knocked over a giant bucket of crystal ore. Rose and I used to huddle up and look into forever, and I'd tell her the names of the stars until her breathing slowed and I knew she was asleep.

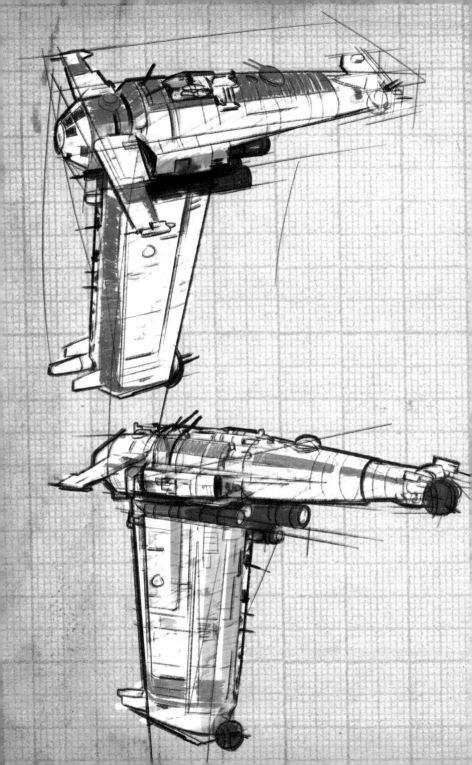

We might have grown up to fly orediggers and blast ice for mining crews, except our world was in First Order territory. The only time you'd see First Order types in person was when their recruiters made the rounds of our villages.

The recruiters wanted geologists and technicians, and they'd pay good money if you'd join up and relocate. "Tame the galactic frontier!" their holos would blare over and over again, with no one quite brave enough to shut them off. But they'd also take children. That was the creepy part. They promised parents that they'd provide food, shelter, and education for any child who signed on to the FrontierCorps.

Mostly the First Order left Hays Minor alone. But then a few years ago they started putting overseers on oredigger runs—grim men and women in dark uniforms, who glowered at everything, but never said a word. They just took notes, and we all got used to them.

GALACTIC MAP

That's one thing I've learned—some of the most dangerous evils are the ones you get used to. It isn't always soldiers coming in the night, at least not at first. Sometimes it starts more quietly.

One day I walked into Central Ridge Mining to find Mama pale and angry. First Order officials were standing in the control room, with stormtroopers for backup. They said production methods had to change, and handed out new procedures for us to follow.

They ordered us to start tearing Hays Minor apart, blasting huge holes in the crust without bothering with safety protocols. The demolition damaged villages and cavern networks, but we were told to follow orders or they'd find someone else who wanted our jobs. The First Order was looking for exotic ores we'd never heard of that weren't in our scan files.

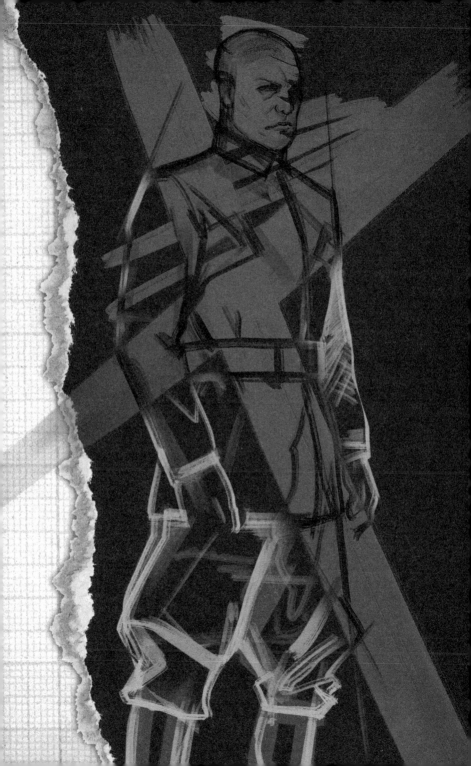

Within a few months they'd taken over almost all the old mining firms and started relocating settlements that were in their way. Those evicted never got a warning. The First Order used those settlements for weapons testing, blasting villages out of existence. Rich beings began landing at Hays Minor's spaceports, flying fancy yachts, and wearing rich furs that must have cost a moon's worth of credits. We learned they were arms dealers, eager to buy and sell new instruments of death and destruction.

That was when our parents started plotting to get me and Rose out of Otomok.

Soon, you could no longer see the stars from our observation dome. The sky was filled with dust, but you could still see the First Order bombers on their way to the weapons test sites. They were gray, bat-winged machines that howled as they passed overhead. I never thought there was a ship I didn't want to fly until I saw that one.

The people of one village, Sebris Gamma, refused to go along with the new orders. The Gammans told the First Order that they'd been an independent mining collective since Republic days and meant to stay that way. We cheered them on—until the First Order bombers came to Sebris Gamma. They dropped ground-penetrating bombs loaded with incendiaries that burned the Gammans alive.

A week after Sebris Gamma, our parents put us on a supply ship to Botajef. When Rose asked if they were coming too, they said they had to stay and fight for Otomok. We told Mama we wanted to fight too, and she said we would, but not there. The fight was bigger than just our homeworld. Papa promised we'd see each other again, then gave us his parents' medallions. This way, he said, Otomok would always be with us—the precious minerals at its heart would sit next to ours.

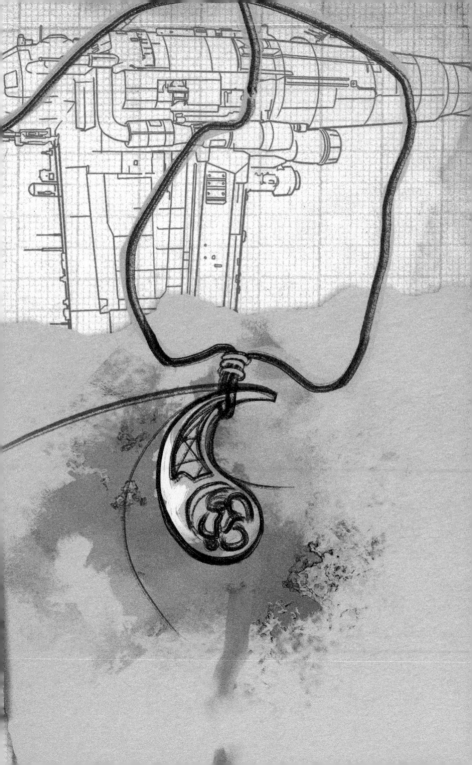

Mama told us to go to a café at Botajef's spaceport, find a Mon Calamari server, and order something not on the menu—the selakale special. An hour later we were on a dingy freighter that brought us to D'Qar and the Resistance. We'd only been there a few days and were still wearing our filtered goggles when Fossil told us our parents were missing.

That same day, the First Order blockaded Otomok. It claimed it was fighting terrorists funded by outside agitators. When the New Republic objected, the First Order said it was an internal matter, which the New Republic accepted! Rose and I were so furious we couldn't see straight. We asked for a meeting with General Organa, but she just looked sad when we explained what had happened. "This is why the Resistance exists," she told us.

Since then we've only had a few reports from Otomok. They say Hays Minor has been depopulated and blasted nearly in two by demolition runs, and that the First Order has launched a military crackdown on Hays Major.

Rose insists Mama and Papa survived and one day we'll be together again back home, but I don't believe that. Besides, it sounds like we no longer have a home to return to. The First Order took ours from us.

Many Resistance members can say the same. The First Order turned Fossil's world, Martaus VI, into a labor camp. Statura fought Imperial stormtroopers as a teenager on Garel. And General Organa had to watch as the Death Star blew up Alderaan. We're fighting not just so people remember Otomok, but so others don't lose their homes, too.

Rose wanted to head straight for the First Order's territory and start blowing things up, and she was disappointed to be told—several times—that it wasn't that simple. The Resistance and the First Order were enemies, but they weren't at war. The New Republic still thought it was possible to live in peace with the First Order, and wouldn't support our efforts.

Or at least not officially. Working in secret, New Republic senators sent us everything from starfighters to intelligence reports. But we had to go about business quietly, without doing anything that the First Order could make into a diplomatic incident.

How do you fight a war quietly?

I'm still trying to figure that one out, to be honest. What the First Order does is brilliant: It secretly pays pirates, slavers, and others to spread terror in star systems near its borders, then steps in to "rescue" the pirates' victims. Except the rescuers never leave, and soon the planets they saved are part of First Order territory.

What we try to do is get there <u>first</u>. When the First Order tried to take over the Cassander sector, in the Borderlands between the New Republic and First Order Space, Rose and I had our first mission.

Pirates have troubled the star systems near the Kalki Nebula for centuries, using bases inside the nebula for hit-and-run attacks. But suddenly, instead of falling-apart converted freighters and old Clone Wars transports, the pirates had brand-news attack ships and heavy weapons, which they used to start raiding Mamkoda and Caraxl.

Our first target was Mamkoda, where the pirates seized a spaceport and fortified it as a base of operations. Fossil sent us out with six bombers: Cobalt Hammer, Scarab, and Wasp in one flight and Crimson Bolide, Dancer, and Hailstorm in the other, accompanied by an A-wing squadron, Cobalt Belle, as the spare bomber, and a transport loaded with magno-charges.

I was in the ball turret, and I was nervous. When the first bandits appeared on my scope, I was terrified that I'd forgotten all my training. But seconds later I was firing, sweat running down my face, and Tallie's A-wings were swooping in to pound our attackers. I even took out a Z-95. I felt like I was firing for all the people back home at Otomok whose lives had been turned upside down by the First Order.

We drove off the first wave of pirates, I heard Nix calling "bombs away" and Cobalt Hammer swerved and shot upward as the magno-charges were deployed. Target destroyed with no losses—just some damage to our starboard sublight engine, and Rose rerouted the power feeds like she'd been doing it her whole life.

Three days later we did a hop to Caraxl. This time we weren't bringing bombs but supplies. We had to cut that run short because Tallie reported that First Order TIEs were on an intercept course. Our orders were to avoid a fight that might cause problems in the New Republic Senate.

Rose was hopping mad, but it was all part of the plan. When we returned to the Ninka, we learned Resistance spies had pinpointed the location of the pirates' base—Sheh Soahi. I don't know how we learned that—someone said something about droids—but the intel was solid.

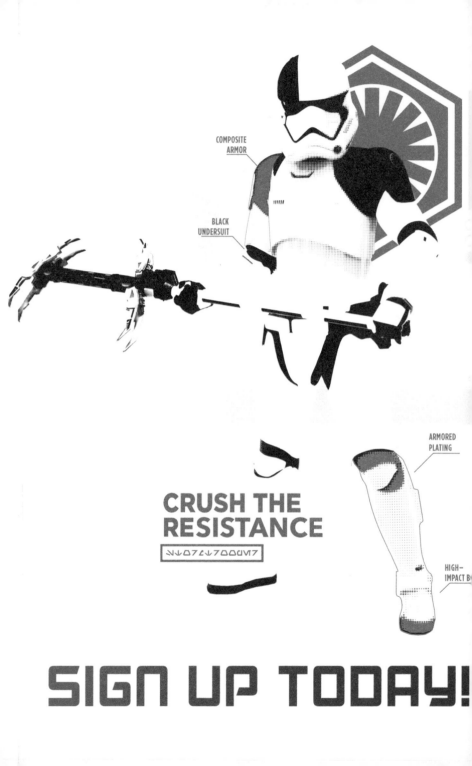

COMPOSITE
ARMOR

BLACK
UNDERSUIT

ARMORED
PLATING

**CRUSH THE
RESISTANCE**

HIGH-
IMPACT B

SIGN UP TODAY!

TAME THE GALACTIC FRONTIER!

EVERY DAY BRAVE SCOUTS FROM THE FIRST ORDER DISCOVER NEW PLANETS BEYOND THE GALACTIC FRONTIER! THESE WORLDS OFFER OPPORTUNITY AND ADVENTURE UNDER THE LEADERSHIP OF THE FIRST ORDER, WITHOUT THE CORRUPTION AND DISORDER THAT INFECTS NEW REPUBLIC PLANETS.

THE FIRST ORDER IS SEEKING SKILLED WORKERS— SCIENTISTS, RESEARCHERS, AND INDUSTRIALISTS— TO HELP ENSURE THE SECURITY AND STRENGTH OF THESE NEW WORLDS.

LACK THESE SKILLS? ENSURE THAT THE NEXT GENERATION WILL HAVE THEM BY ENROLLING YOUR CHILDREN IN THE FRONTIERCORPS. CHILDREN APPROVED WILL BE GUARANTEED FOOD, SHELTER, EDUCATION, AND THE OPPORTUNITY TO MAKE THE GALAXY A BETTER PLACE.

FIRST
ORDER

Sheh Soahi was a tough fight. The pirates sent everything up against us. Cobalt Scarab's front deflector failed and it had to withdraw, but Cobalt Belle slotted into the hole in the formation and we stayed on target. We lost two A-wings, but turned that pirate base to slag. Even better, we intercepted transmissions from Sheh Soahi's pirates demanding help from the First Order . . . recordings that ought to be of great interest to the New Republic Senate.

When we returned, I felt like we'd earned our place and were making a difference. I guess General Organa thought so too, because she had a new mission for us—a run to Atterra to spy on the First Order.

The general had heard of Rose's wizardry with a Harris wrench, so she asked my kid sister to come up with a way to turn a bomber into a spy ship. Rose was really nervous about whether she could do what the general wanted, and kept insisting there were a lot of flight engineers who could think of something better. She was wrong, of course. I made her record what she did, and one of these days I'm going to make her explain it to me.

ROSE'S MODIFICATIONS

Paige wanted me to write about the modifications I made to our bomber to escape detection on the run to Atterra. All I did was mess around with some tools. And I'm worried this might jinx us on our next run. But she insisted . . .

I couldn't believe it when General Organa came to me to discuss the spy mission she wanted to send to Atterra. I mean, she's the commander of the entire Resistance, and I'm just a flight engineer on a bomber.

This is embarrassing, but my first reaction was to ask her about a cloaking device. She just smiled and waited for me to figure out what I should have known in the first place . . . if the Resistance could afford cloaking devices, we wouldn't be stuck trying to use bombers as spy ships.

So, I got to work on the problem. Right away I realized there was no way to make us invisible, but what I could do was make the energy output from a bomber look like trace emissions that wouldn't light up an enemy sensor scope.

The first step was to attach baffles to the engines, diffusing the ion exhaust to the sides as well as to the rear. Our spy probes use a similar system, so I just had to figure out how to make it work for something a lot bigger than a probe.

The main problem with my idea was that a bomber puts out a lot more energy than a probe. Even with the baffles doing their thing, we'd stick out like a fathier in a petting zoo. I scrounged up some scrapped auxiliary fuel tanks and emergency shunts and had the ground crew weld them together to attach to the baffles. The tanks capture some of the ion exhaust, hold it, and then bleed it out so it looks like a remnant trace from some ship that passed by days before.

But then—new problem! It was too difficult to control the rate of emissions by hand, even if you didn't have anything else to do during a flight. If that got messed up, the ions could burst the tank or melt it, possibly taking down the engines as well. Then we'd be dead in space, and pretty soon after that, a First Order ship would find us and we'd be dead for real.

I thought about that one a while and decided I needed a helper. We didn't have people to spare so I made a helper. I found an astromech brain waiting for a new body and a flight computer from a scrapped X-wing, wired them together, and convinced them that they needed to talk with each other. They didn't want to do it; it was bending their programming, but I told them I could stick them back on the shelf and that did the trick.

It turned out the biggest part of the job was yet to come. Most of a StarFortress's systems were designed to work on their own, without asking permission from some pesky flight engineer or droid. I had to rig up power plugs and attach them to the systems hub on the flight deck, between my station and Spennie's turret. The plugs interrupt those system processes and let the droid brain and the flight computer control the emissions. When I was done, I'd built this weird thing that was half-droid and half-computer, with about a million wires running from it through the systems hub to the conduits. I call it the baffler . . . and it works!

OK, it *mostly* works. The baffler's power plugs pop out of alignment if you even look at them funny, I'm the only one who can talk to it, and my little monster takes up so much of the flight-deck corridor that Spennie wants to wring my neck every time she has to squeeze past it. But so far the baffler's done its job. Now I'm just crossing my fingers and hoping that doesn't change.

I like to call the baffler the Resistance-cloak—a poor but functional version of the real thing. That's something I'm learning about the Resistance. We can't afford "perfect," so we try and get to "better." If it comes to war with the First Order, we're going to need every little advantage we can get.

REEVE PANZORO

So with the cloak, we flew solo to Atterra and released spy probes over Atterra Alpha and Atterra Bravo. Everyone was holding their breath hoping Rose's crazy contraption would keep the First Order from finding us. They didn't, but someone else did—a starfighter piloted by Reeve and Casca Panzoro, two Atterran rebels. They were so desperate to escape Atterra that Reeve flew his fighter right into Nix's bomb bay, coming within a sonar swallow's flight feather of shearing my ball turret in two.

We brought the Panzoros back to D'Qar so General Organa could hear their story. She sent us back with Reeve aboard a civilian transport to see for ourselves what was happening on Bravo.

We saw something terrible: The First Order was disposing of bodies by dumping them into Bravo's acid sea. They flew people into orbit without oxygen, and their lives were erased in just hours.

General Organa has seen more evil than I can imagine, but she was angry enough to approve a plan to send our bombers back to Atterra with supplies for Bravo Rising, the Panzoros' resistance group.

Rose nearly dropped from exhaustion rigging bafflers, but she got it done. We went to Refnu, where we could pose as temp workers on ice-breaking duty, and prepared to make four supply runs to Atterra.

CASCA PANZORO

On the first run we were spotted by TIEs. They swooped in on us and this time we knew we had to fight, whatever diplomatic incident it might cause. I blasted one of those arrogant little space spiders, then another, and then a third!

Unfortunately, one of the TIEs got away, and on our second run they were waiting for us. That was one of the worst days of my life—Cobalt Hornet, Scarab, and Wasp were destroyed, with all their crewers lost.

Still, we knew we had to go back. This time, the bombers arrived in pairs, with an empty one serving as a decoy to distract the TIEs, while the full bomber made the supply drop to Atterra. It worked! We came back to Refnu with a couple of cracked blast shields, but nothing that couldn't be fixed.

But on the way back from that hop, something strange happened: some kind of cosmic shock wave interfered with our systems. We argued about what it might be, but there was no obvious answer. Whatever it was, it was traveling faster than light speed.

I got to fly on the final run to Atterra, and I was so nervous I was sure Tiggs would ground me. Coming out of hyperspace, I expected to find space full of TIEs, and I wasn't sure if I wanted to be in the cockpit trying to dodge them or in my ball turret where I could shoot them.

But there weren't any TIEs. The last supply drop was a complete milk run. It was like the First Order had forgotten about us.

When we got back to Refnu, we learned the terrible truth. That disruption in hyperspace was from a First Order superweapon that had destroyed the New Republic capital of Hosnian Prime and the entire leadership. Our pilots had taken out the weapon, but the Resistance was now at war with the First Order—and badly outgunned.

My reaction after seeing the mission briefing about the raid on the First Order's so-called Starkiller Base? I felt guilty. We lost many brave pilots trying to crack the weapon's oscillator with laser cannons that weren't designed for that kind of target. Our bombers could have blown a hole in it, but we weren't there ... we were at Atterra.

And I wasn't the only one who felt that way. When Vice-Admiral Holdo gave us our new orders, she told us not to blame ourselves for failing to stop an evil we couldn't have known about, particularly since we were trying to do good elsewhere. She said we should dedicate ourselves to creating the best possible future.

And that future starts now. The First Order traced our starfighters back to D'Qar, and it's their next target. We've got the Ninka, eight bombers, and an escort squadron of X-wings and A-wings. We're going to race the First Order to D'Qar and hope we arrive first.

I'll be in the ball turret when we come out of hyperspace at D'Qar. But for the first time, I won't be flying with my sister. Holdo requested that Rose join her aboard the Ninka, telling her that she needed her expertise. And once we reach D'Qar, General Organa wants Rose to serve aboard her cruiser.

Rose agreed to go even though she didn't want to. I'm proud of her for that, even though I wish she was here with me.

The ball turret feels strangely large without her.

Paige transmitted this to me while the Ninka was in hyperspace on the way to D'Qar. Now it's all I have left of her.

Paige Tico—citizen of Otomok, pilot and gunner in the Resistance, and my big sister—was killed in the evacuation of D'Qar. Before she died, Cobalt Hammer delivered the payload that destroyed a First Order dreadnought and allowed General Organa to escape. She died the same way she lived . . . as a hero.

I can't believe I had to write those words. I don't want to believe they're true.

But they are. Now the First Order is tracking us, seeking to destroy what's left of our Resistance.

But they won't do it.

I swear it on my own medallion—whose twin was lost with Paige.

I swear it on the memory of my sister, everything she fought for, and everything she taught me.

I'm Rose Tico, and I swear I'll find a way to defeat the First Order.

For Otomok.

For freedom.

And for you, Paige.

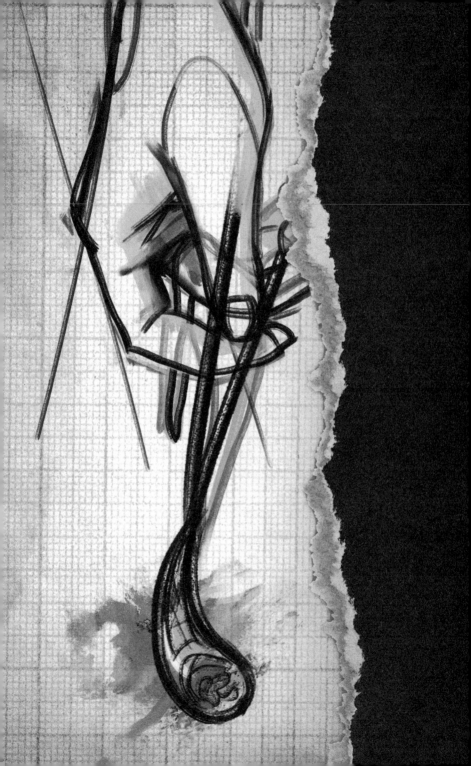

Studio Fun International
An imprint of Printers Row Publishing Group
A division of Readerlink Distribution Services, LLC
10350 Barnes Canyon Road, Suite 100, San Diego, CA 92121
www.studiofun.com

Written by Jason Fry
Illustrated by Cyril Nouvel
Designed by Kara Kenna

All notations of errors or omissions should be addressed to Studio Fun International,
Editorial Department, at the above address.

ISBN: 978-0-7944-4084-8

Manufactured, printed, and assembled in Stevens Point, WI, United States of America.

First printing, September 2017. WOR/09/17

21 20 19 18 17 1 2 3 4 5

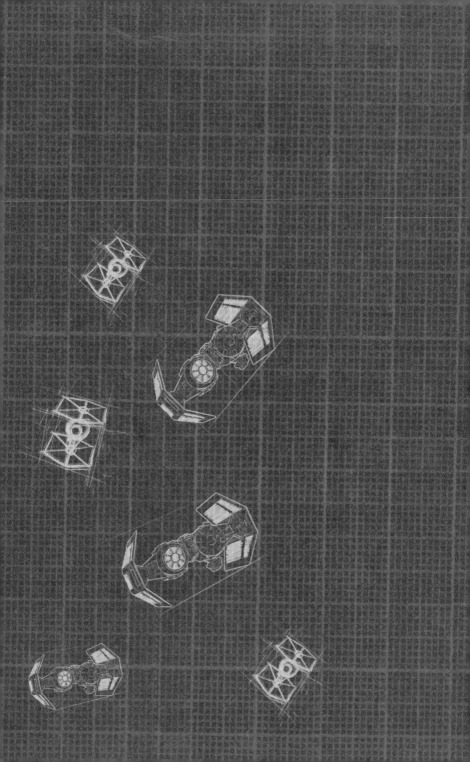